Dear Parents:

Ready Reader Storybooks™ have been developed with your kinder-
garten through second-grader in mind. This series is designed to
encourage young readers to begin to read alone, thus increasing basic
reading skills. The simple stories have easy-to-follow plots, and the
bright, colorful illustrations add to the fun, and provide the visual
appeal that helps to promote and enhance your youngster's reading
experience.

The stories in this series vary in subject matter and style, so your
child will be sure to find stories of interest. The large type is easy to
read, and the format is just the right size for small hands to hold.
The Ready Reader Storybooks™ will delight while developing and
encouraging your child's independent reading skills.

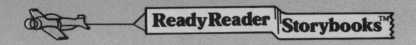

Patty for President

Written by Jean Davis Callaghan

Illustrated by Mary Ann Fraser

Modern Publishing
A Division of Unisystems, Inc.
New York, New York 10022

Penelope and Patty are twins.

They are in the second grade.

Friday, the class will vote for the class president.

"Who will you vote for?"
Penelope asks Patty.

"For myself," says Patty. "I want to be president."

Patty tells everyone, "Vote for me for president."

Bossy Patty tells Penelope, "I want you to be my helper. Go get some cookies and pass them out. Say they are from me."

"Also, I want you to help everyone with their homework, and tell them it was my idea."

Penelope doesn't like being bossed around, but she does love her sister.

So she bakes cookies and hands
them out to the class.

The class likes the cookies so much, Patty asks Penelope to bring them every day.

During recess, and after school, Penelope helps the other students with their homework.

It bothers Penelope that Patty is so bossy, but Penelope keeps working hard for her sister.

Penelope works so hard that she gets tired. One day, she almost falls asleep in class.

Patty doesn't do any work. She only sits on the swing, talking and laughing–

and eating the cookies that
Penelope made!

Meanwhile, Penelope works hard to make Patty the second-grade class president.

At last it is Friday.

The teacher says, "It's time for the class to vote."

Everyone waits to see who will get the most votes.

The teacher says, "The class president is…

...Penelope!"

Penelope wins because the class thinks she is a kind person, and a hard worker.